WE ADOPTED YOU, BENJAMIN KOO

Linda Walvoord Girard
Illustrated by Linda Shute

Albert Whitman & Company, Morton Grove, Illinois

Special thanks to Betsy Guinn, Director of Special Needs Adoptions,
and Anne Krush, Special Services, Holt International Children's Services.

Library of Congress Cataloging-in-Publication Data
Girard, Linda Walvoord.
  We adopted you, Benjamin Koo / Linda Walvoord Girard; illustrated by Linda Shute.
    p. cm.
  Summary: Nine-year-old Benjamin Koo Andrews, adopted from Korea as an infant, describes
what it's like to grow up adopted from another country.
  ISBN 0-8075-8694-3 (hardcover). ISBN 0-8075-8695-1 (paperback).
  1. Andrews, Benjamin Koo—Juvenile literature.   2. Children, Adopted—Korea (South)—
Biography—Juvenile literature.   3. Intercountry adoption—United States—Biography—Juvenile
literature.   4. Interracial adoption—United States—Biography—Juvenile literature. [1. Adoption.
2. Korean Americans.] I. Shute, Linda, ill. II. Title.
HV875.55.G57   1989   88-23653
362.7'34'0924—dc19   CIP
[B]   AC

Design by Karen Yops.

This book is for Benjamin,
who shared his thoughts
in order to help
other adopted children. L.W.G.

For Laura Sun and Julianna Rose
and their proud parents. L.S.

My name is Benjamin Koo Andrews. I'm nine years old, but I don't know when my real birthday is.

No one knows my real birthday except my first mother, in Korea. When I was about ten days old, she left me on the step of an orphanage there. That cold stone doorstep where I was found one chilly evening in October is where my story begins.

Sometimes at night I think about my past. Why did my birthmother leave me there? Was she sad when she put me on that step? Was I cold?

I was bundled up well, and the people at the orphanage found me soon. I'll never meet my birthmother, but I know she didn't leave me just anyplace. She left me where she knew loving people could find me easily. I think she really cared about me.

On the day they found me, the workers gave me a name and a birthday. They guessed my birthday was about October 10, so that's on all my records. The name they gave me was Koo Hyun Soo, which means "flower found by water." Today part of that name is still mine—I'm Benjamin Koo Andrews.

Now comes the happy part of my story. The orphanage was trying to find parents for each baby, and far away in America, my mother and father were waiting and hoping that a baby could be found for them.

One day a worker at the orphanage took my picture. Then she wrote this about me: "Baby Hyun Soo is alert and cries a lot; he appears healthy, but he is very tiny. He grasps at sunlight when it crosses his crib. He kicks very strongly."

My picture and the description were sent to my mom and dad. "This baby needs you," the letter said.

When my mom got the letter, she was so happy that she cried. She carried that picture in her purse for months and showed it to everyone she and Dad knew—their families, friends, and the people they worked with. Mom even brought the picture to the kids she taught in first grade. "This baby is coming from Korea to be our new baby!" she told them.

But then my parents waited. So did I. When you're being adopted from a foreign place, there are all sorts of papers to be filled out.

It was hard for my parents to wait. "I didn't want to miss a single day of your life!" Mom says.

The orphanage wrote another letter. It asked my parents to send lots of money—thousands of dollars. Mom and Dad had to pay for my plane trip and for a lady who would bring me to America and take care of me on the way. You can't mail a baby like a football in a box!

Finally, in April, came the great day I call America Day. That day, with other babies, I flew clear across the huge Pacific Ocean to America. The helpers wrapped me up—in a pink outfit! In Korea, pink doesn't mean girl, and blue doesn't mean boy. They just use whatever nice clothes they have.

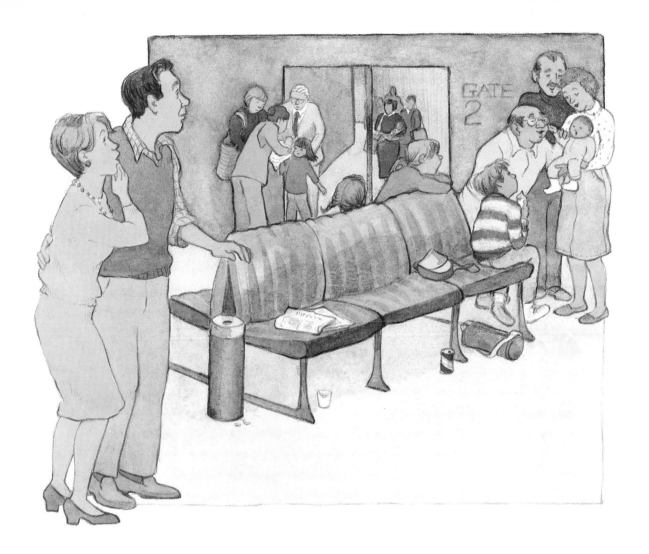

At the airport, my mom and dad held their breath as the other babies came off with their helpers and were given to their parents for the first time. Each worker would say, "Where are Tommy's parents?" or "Where are Emily's parents?" Grandmothers and uncles and brothers and sisters crowded around each little bundle.

My mom and dad watched until the very last baby came off the plane. My mother almost started to cry. That couldn't be their baby! Koo Hyun Soo was a boy, and here came the last baby, in pink!

But the helper looked at them. "Benjamin's parents?" she asked. Dad shouted, "Yes!" and Mom rushed up and took me in her arms. Then, still afraid there'd been a mix-up, she reached down and checked under my clothes! In spite of the pink outfit, I was a boy.

Everything had turned out all right. The ocean might be big, I might be little, I might be last—but I was here.

My parents made up for lost time by cuddling me, playing with me, and giving me the kind of food I needed to grow. By my first birthday, I wasn't skinny anymore!

I don't remember the day we went to court for my adoption because I was fourteen months old. A baby adopted to America can become a citizen, so four months later I became an American.

When I was little, I didn't think about who I was; I was moving too fast most of the time. Sometimes my mom wished there were speed limits for tricycles! I loved the highest swings, the tallest slides, and big family parties. I got to know my three grandparents, five uncles, four aunts, and all my cousins. I felt part of a family. To me, we were all the same.

My parents started early telling me I was adopted. My mom is a first-grade teacher, so she knows how to explain things to little kids. But when Mom and Dad said I had a birthmother, it didn't really mean anything. "We adopted you from Korea" sounded no different than "Uncle Jack was born in Pittsburgh."

When I went to nursery school, I used to draw pictures of myself and my family. I colored my hair black and my skin light brown, the way I'd color a lake blue or the sun yellow. I had noticed my looks, but I didn't think about them. I felt I was just like everyone around me.

Then one morning when I was in second grade, I was combing my hair, and my hand just stopped. I stared at myself in the mirror. I saw that I was Korean! I was different from my parents! I laugh now when I think how surprised I was at that moment.

I watched in school all day for one other face like mine, but no one looked like me.

All of a sudden, my looks mattered a lot to me. How
can you feel like your mother's child when you don't look
like her at all? I began to wonder who my birthmother was,
and if I had any brothers or sisters. I asked my parents a lot
of questions, but they knew very little about my early life.

I had some pictures of Korea that a soldier friend had brought. But the pictures made me feel sad. I didn't want to look at snow-capped mountains in Korea. I wanted to know who my mother was.

I began to feel angry because other kids knew their biological families, and I never would. One time, when my mom made me obey a rule, I got mad. "I'm leaving!" I shouted. "I'm going back to Korea! I'll find my real mother, and she'll be nice to me!"

My mom stayed calm. "You have a real mom, and that's me," she said. "I know you're upset, but you have to mind my rules."

I started to run away. I really did. Then I realized I'd get to the end of the sidewalk, and I wouldn't know which way Korea was!

That night Dad hugged me and said he was glad I had decided to stay. But I still felt like I was on the sidewalk, not sure where to turn.

During second grade, I talked to Mrs. James. She's our counselor at school. She's there to talk to, and nothing a kid says can ever hurt her feelings. I told her I didn't have a real mom. She told me a joke about a duck. She said, "How do you know a duck is a duck?" I said I didn't know.

"Well," she said, "if it walks like a duck and quacks like a duck and acts like a duck, then it *is* a duck. And whoever talks like a mom and loves you like a mom and stands behind you like a mom *is* your mom." I felt better then.

I told my mom the duck story, and she laughed. Now, once in a while when we hug, we both say, "Quack, quack."

Mrs. James and I talked about my dad, too. I told her how he'd given me a really soft catcher's mitt that he broke in when he was a kid. It has "Andrews" scratched in it. He didn't give it to anyone else. He saved it for me.

After that, I thought about the duck or my mitt when I felt mixed up. It didn't make things perfect, but it helped sometimes. Second grade was a hard year, but I got through it.

The next year, when I was eight, our family took a new step. One night we were eating spaghetti in a restaurant. Suddenly Dad said, "Ben, we have something to talk over."

I thought he meant I had to shape up about something. But no. My mom and dad were thinking of adopting a baby girl from Brazil. A daughter for them, a sister for me. "Would you like to be a big brother?" Mom asked.

I said I'd like a sister, but inside I wasn't sure.

A social worker visited our house and even interviewed me. The agency has to be careful when they choose a family for a baby.

It took months to get the papers filled out so we could adopt Susan. All that time, I wondered about her. I knew what she looked like because a picture of a tiny girl had arrived in a letter. Susan was three, and she was thin.

When my parents flew to Brazil to get Susan, I stayed with my grandma. I remember Mom and Dad came back late one night with my new sister. She had lots of black hair and big, dark eyes. I hugged her—very carefully. I was still sleepy, and so was she, but she smiled at me.

For the first few weeks, Susan was shy. I was the first one in the family who got her to giggle.

When Susan's adoption was final, I went to court with my family. I wore a tie. The judge asked my parents, "Do you promise to love this child for always and to take care of her until she's all grown up?"

"We do," they said.

Then he asked me if I would promise to be her brother always. I said, "Yes."

"Very good," said the judge, and he signed the paper. He didn't care where any of us were born. Our promises made us a family.

Now that she's four, Susan can be a pain, but she's my sister and I'm her brother. We'll stick together.

Our friends and relatives don't find our family weird, but sometimes strangers act dumb. Once at the supermarket a lady saw me, then Susan, then my mom come around the corner. She looked us over.

"Are they yours?" she asked my mom. She didn't even look at Susan and me. She spoke as if we were doorknobs.

"Yes," Mom said.

"Are they brother and sister? I mean, did they come from the same family?"

My mom winked at me. "They're *in* the same family," she said. She put her arm around me and gently made Susan stop bouncing on the cart.

"Oh," said the lady.

Mom says that sometimes we have to help people learn. America is full of all different sorts of families.

And America is full of people who weren't born where they live right now. My dad says a birthplace is just a place to start.

I'm not sad anymore when I think about Korea. Korea feels like a place I don't know that's still "mine." I have a big map of Korea on the wall of my room, and I've read some books Mom bought me about the country. On the Korean New Year, we have a party at home. We eat with chopsticks and sing a song with words that were hard to learn. It's about mountains and the sky—it's a song Korean children sing.

For Susan, we celebrate Carnival. That's a holiday time in Brazil. We try dancing the samba, and we dress up in costumes like the Brazilians do. Susan thinks our party is fun though she doesn't really understand why it's for her.

Our parents want to share everything about me and Susan, not forget the past or try to erase it like a mistake.

I do have one problem. It's the kids at school. Fourth grade can be tough. A few kids call me "Chink" when they tease. Some people don't want to know anything about me. They just think I'm from Afghanistan or Hawaii or Timbuktu.

"I don't like him," I heard a girl say. "He's Japanese."

"Yeah, but watch out—he probably knows karate," said the other kid.

I don't know karate, and I'm not Japanese. It hurts when kids tease me or talk about me like I'm an alien from the moon.

I can answer the teasers with a fact: I'm an American. Or else I can be friendly and say, "I was born in Korea. Where were you born?" Sometimes my best bet is to ignore people when they're being mean. And I've learned to concentrate on my good friends, the kids who like me the way I am.

Wait until Susan gets to fourth grade. I'll be a big eighth grader by then. Dad and I joke that we *will* take up karate if anyone gives Susan a tough time.

I'll never know anything about my birthmother, and that will always hurt a little. But I'm pretty happy with my life. I have parents and a sister and grandparents and aunts and uncles who really love me. I have lots of friends. And I guess I can handle a few mean kids at school.

I just do the best I can. Today I'm in the fastest classes they have in our town for kids in the fourth grade. And I'm a good runner. Lots of Koreans are. I hope someday I'll be a star in soccer or track and maybe an engineer. No matter who you are or where you came from, there's no telling what you can do.

I'm hoping to visit Korea someday, and my parents say they'll help me do that when I'm eighteen. Right now, though, I'm saving for a skateboard.

If you're adopted, ask all the questions you want to. Your parents will tell you what they know, even if part of your story is sad. If you ended up safe and taken care of, it probably means your birthmother did the best she could for you, and so did some other people you'll never meet. But that's in the past. Right now, your name is your name, and your family is your family. You might have been born somewhere else or look different from your parents, but that has nothing to do with love. Take it from me. I'm Benjamin Koo Andrews. I'm nine, and I know.